# DON'T GET CAUGHT

# IN THE TEACHERS' LOUNGE

## Other books by Todd Strasser

# DON'T GET CAUGHT IN THE TEACHERS' LOUNGE

## TODD STRASSER

---
AN
APPLE
PAPERBACK

SCHOLASTIC INC.

New York   Toronto   London   Auckland   Sydney
Mexico City   New Delhi   Hong Kong   Buenos Aires

ISBN 0-439-21065-8

Copyright © 2001 by Todd Strasser. All rights reserved. Published by Scholastic Inc. SCHOLASTIC, APPLE PAPERBACKS, and associated logos are trademarks and/or registered trademarks of Scholastic Inc.

12 11 10 9 8 7 6 5 4 3                    1 2 3 4 5 6/0

Printed in the U.S.A.                    40

First Scholastic printing, December 2001

*To Tom and Arthur*

Hi, this is Kyle Brawly. Maybe you know me from the other *Don't Get Caught* books. Maybe you don't. If you read this book, you're going to find out that my friends Dusty, Wilson, and I mess around a lot. But we never get caught, no matter what we're up to. We're really expert at slipping through the long, sticky fingers of authority. Except in our case they're the short, grubby fingers of Monkey Breath, the weirdest middle-school principal who ever lived.

There's nothing Grubby Fingers Monkey Breath would like more than to nail us doing something wrong and throw us into permanent suspension.

Up till now that's never happened. Then again, up till now we've never been involved in a scam quite like the one Dusty's come up with, either. Don't ask me why Wilson and I are going to go along with this one. We should probably have our heads examined.

"**H**urry up, guys, I have to show you something in the teachers' lounge," said Dusty.

It was lunchtime, and my friends and I were sitting at our usual table. Wilson had just finished eating dessert (he always eats dessert first). Now he was doing the old dip 'n' lick with a french fry and a big blob of ketchup. Wilson's sort of short and pudgy and innocent-looking, which makes him perfect for our scams.

I was trying to chew on a rubbery cheeseburger.

"Come again?" I said, certain I had not heard Dusty right.

"There's something you guys have to see in the teachers' lounge." Dusty stretched his long, thin frame and jerked his thumb toward the cafeteria doors.

"Uh, dude, need I remind you that the teachers' lounge is strictly, totally, and absopositively off-limits to kids?" I said. "We get caught in there, and Monkey Breath will skin us alive."

As I mentioned earlier, Monkey Breath was our principal. His real name was Mr. Chump, and he was one seriously sick puppy.

"*If* we get caught," Dusty stressed.

"Why do you want to go into the teachers' lounge anyway?" asked Wilson as he licked the ketchup off another fry.

"Because it's the only place in school that has a soda machine," answered Dusty. "*And* the sodas cost only *a third* of what we pay in the store."

I lowered my cheeseburger and stared at him. "Dude, have you forgotten the *numero uno* rule in this school?"

"No soda," Dusty replied.

"So going into the *teachers' lounge* to get *a soda* is like hitting the top spot on the FBI's Most Wanted list," Wilson surmised.

"I thought our mission was to only break the rules Monkey Breath hasn't thought of yet," I said.

Dusty smiled mysteriously. "We'll get to that."

I was just about to ask what he meant when Wilson whispered, *"Look out."*

Dusty and I twisted around.

Alice Appleford was coming toward us.

And she looked really, *really* upset.

**3**

Alice is president of the student government. She has straight, shoulder-length blond hair that is always perfect and she almost always wears skirts to school and sometimes even dresses. She also wears glasses even though Wilson says there's nothing wrong with her eyes. He thinks she wears them because she thinks they make her look smart.

At that moment Alice looked more upset than smart. Her forehead was wrinkled and her lips were pressed down in a pout. You knew something truly strange was going on because she actually sat down at our table. She'd never done that before.

Wilson dipped a french fry in ketchup and held it out to her. "Dip 'n' lick?"

Alice stuck out her tongue. "Gross 'n' disgusting."

"Don't knock it till you've tried it," Wilson said.

Alice ignored him and turned to Dusty and me. "Look, guys, we have a major crisis."

"The cheerleaders can't find their pom-poms?" Dusty guessed.

"No," said Alice.

"The gym teachers can't find their whips?" I guessed.

Alice shook her head.

"Someone left the screen door on the submarine open?" asked Wilson.

Alice frowned at him. "No, we are in serious danger of losing our chance to go to Big Splash."

Big Splash is an awesome water park. If our school, Hart Marks, won the districtwide recycling competition, we'd get a free trip *and* a day off from school.

"My spies tell me Jeffersonville is just about tied with us in recycling," Alice explained. "If they win, they go to Big Splash instead of us."

Jeffersonville was the next town over. The Burt Ipchupt Middle School there was our biggest rival.

"If they win, they deserve to go," I pointed out.

Alice's eyed widened in horror. "They are *not* going to win. We are *not* going to let them! We can't lose. Hart Marks Middle School does not accept failure."

"This isn't about winning or losing," I tried to

remind her. "It's about recycling. It's about trying to save the environment. I mean, sure, we'd like to go to Big Splash, but the important thing is that we recycle even if we don't get to go."

Alice balled her hands into fists and leaned across the table. "Listen to me, Kyle Brawly, I know you like to make fun of how competitive I am, but this is a matter of school pride. Those jerks at Burp It Up *cannot* be allowed to beat us."

"How can we stop them?" Wilson asked.

Alice pointed a finger at me. Her fingernail was painted red with a little yellow flower in the middle. "The only way we're going to win is if *you* help, Kyle."

"Why me?" I asked.

"Because everyone in this school looks up to you," Dusty said in a teasing voice.

"You're our hero, Kyle." Wilson batted his eyelashes.

"Everyone *does* look up to Kyle," Alice said. "Especially boys. If they knew you were helping with the recycling competition, they'd help, too. You see Mr. Recycling Box?"

Alice pointed across the cafeteria at a large green cardboard box with the words MR. RECYCLING BOX written on the side.

"No one's put a thing in that box for the past two days." Alice handed me an empty plastic salad container. "Why don't you put this in and see what happens?"

"It's a trick, Kyle," Dusty warned me. "Don't do it."

"The box is booby-trapped," added Wilson. "If you go near it, it'll spray you with mustard."

In spite of their warnings, I decided to see what would happen. I went over to Mr. Recycling Box and threw in the empty salad container. Then I went back to the table and sat down.

"So what was the point of that?" Dusty asked.

"Just watch," said Alice.

We all watched Mr. Recycling Box. After a few moments, a sixth grader threw in a juice bottle. Then an eighth grader threw in some foil, and a seventh grader tossed in the plastic from a Lunchable.

"See?" Alice said, as if she thought she'd proved her point. "Not only is that the first time in two days that anyone's recycled anything, but it's the first time in more than a week that a boy's done it. In fact, they were all boys. And do you want to guess why they suddenly decided to recycle?"

"Because a little voice in their head told them to?" Wilson guessed.

"No," said Alice. "Because they saw Kyle do it."

I expected my friends to argue and was surprised when they didn't.

"Okay, maybe you're right," Dusty admitted. "But what do you want Kyle to do? Put something in Mr. Recycling Box every three minutes just to get other kids to do it?"

"No," answered Alice. "I have a much better way of getting him to help our cause." She turned to me. "All you have to do is be my co-anchor on the morning TV show and *tell* them to recycle. Everyone in school will see you, and they'll all listen."

"Not this again," I groaned.

Every morning, Alice hosted the world's most boring morning school news show on Hart TV. For weeks she'd been begging me to be her co-anchor. I tried to imagine myself sitting next to Alice at the news desk.

Everyone in school would see me on TV every morning. . . .

I'd feel important. . . .

I'd rattle off the school announcements and all the other dumb stuff we heard day after day. . . .

Then again, I could just hang upside down from the school's flagpole.

Everyone would still get to see me. . . .

But at least I wouldn't have to do announcements. . . .

"I think I'll pass," I said.

Alice's face fell. "At least say you'll help with the recycling."

Before I could answer, the cafeteria PA crackled on: *"Dustin Lane, Wilson Kriss, and Kyle Brawly, report to the office immediately."*

My friends and I got up.

"Sorry, Alice," I said. "Looks like I've been called away."

**5**

There was nothing unusual about my friends and me being called down to the office. It happened about once a week. Only most of the time we knew why.

"Anyone know what we did wrong this time?" Dusty calmly asked as we walked down the hall toward the office. Our nickname for him is King Calm. Nothing seems to worry him.

"Not a clue," I replied.

"We must've done *something*," Wilson fretted.

"Hey, look," someone called out. "It's Moe, Larry, and Curly."

I knew the voice before I saw the big mouth it came out of. It was Gary Gordon, the biggest double-jerk-face eighth grader in school.

"What are you guys in trouble for now?" Gary asked.

"Knowing toads like you," answered Dusty.

"All right!" Wilson, Dusty, and I slapped palms.

"You guys are just half a laugh," Gary grumbled.

"We'd rather be half a laugh than a total rump-scrubbing kiss-up like you," I shot back.

Gary gave us a nasty smile. "You guys think you're so smart. Like you're such big rebellious outlaws and you're never gonna follow the rules. Well, let me tell you something. You may think I'm a kiss-up, but in the long run you guys are gonna be burger flippers at McDonald's. Meanwhile, I'm gonna make something of myself."

"Sure," Dusty cracked. "You'll make it all the way to a McDonald's assistant manager."

Gary's mouth fell open. "That's not what I meant!"

But it was too late. My friends and I laughed and continued toward the school office. Dusty strolled along with his head high and a smile on his face like he didn't have a care in the world. Wilson trudged with his head down and his hands jammed in his pockets. He was seriously worried.

"I bet Monkey Breath knows we were planning to sneak into the teachers' lounge," he said.

"Right." Dusty chuckled. "He can read our minds."

"What if he's hidden a mike under our lunch table or something?" Wilson asked.

I put my hand on Wilson's forehead. It was cool. "He's not running a fever."

"I'm *serious*," Wilson insisted.

"Just chill," Dusty advised. "Whatever Monkey Breath wants, we'll deal with it."

We got to the office. Inside, our assistant principal, Ms. Ivana Fortune, was talking to Mr. Gutsy, the gym teacher. Ms. Fortune is the world's only babe assistant principal. She has red hair and red lips and wears tight dresses and high heels. Mr. Gutsy is tall and skinny and bald. We always see them whispering in the halls and giving each other gooey-eyed looks. They also exercise together after school in the Weight and Exercise room.

Just about everyone in school knows they have a big-time "love among teachers" thing going. We all agree it's major league gross.

But today something was different. Their whispers and gooey-eyed looks had been replaced with frowns and wrinkled foreheads. When my friends and I went into the office, Mr. Gutsy stopped speaking to Ms. Fortune and left. Ms. Fortune turned to us. Her lips were in a straight, hard line.

"You're here to see Principal Chump?" she asked.

"Who else?" I answered.

Ms. Fortune leaned close and spoke in a low

voice as if she didn't want anyone to hear. "Try not to do or say anything that might upset him, okay? Just be cooperative."

"Why?" asked Dusty.

"He's . . ." Our assistant principal hesitated. "Let's just say he's a little under the weather."

One of the office phones rang, and Ms. Fortune turned to answer it. My friends and I shared a puzzled look.

"What does 'under the weather' mean?" Wilson whispered.

"Like, he's not feeling well, or something," I answered.

"Hey, check out his new door," Dusty said.

Wilson and I looked at what used to be the plain wooden door that led to the dark dungeon of the evil Dr. Monkey Breath. Only instead of the wooden door there was now a thick gray metal door with huge, shiny steel hinges. At eye level was a small, rectangular slot.

The slot slid open, and a pair of wild, bloodshot eyes appeared on the other side. It was Monkey Breath. "Who's there?"

"Kyle, Dusty, and Wilson," I answered.

"Why?" our principal asked.

"Uh, you sent for us, remember?" I said.

"I did? Oh, yes, maybe I did." From inside the office came clicking sounds as locks were opened.

*Screeeak!* The door opened just wide enough for our principal to stick out his head and big ears. Monkey Breath craned his neck and looked around as if to make sure no one else was out there. Then he opened the door a little bit wider.

"Come in, boys. Quickly!"

# 6

We hurried into his private office. *Clank!* Monkey Breath slammed the metal door behind us.

*Scrank!* He shoved a big metal bolt closed.

My friends and I looked around. Normally we would have sat down. But then, normally there wasn't a big airport-type metal detector standing just inside the door.

"Wait a second!" Monkey Breath rushed around the detector and sat on a stool in front of the TV/metal detector screen. "Okay, boys, step through."

One at a time, we stepped through the metal detector. No bells or sirens went off. Then we sat down in our usual seats. Monkey Breath sat down at his desk. The walls of his office were covered with gray egg-crate soundproofing. The shades were drawn. The dim room was lit by a single lamp.

Monkey Breath's hair was a mess, and his chin

16

was covered with dark stubble. His eyes were sunken and there were dark rings under them. His black suit was wrinkled and splotched with stains, and his collar was open. He looked like he hadn't slept or changed clothes in days.

"Okay, what are you boys up to now?" he growled.

"Nothing," said Dusty.

Monkey Breath let out a big sigh. That was the worst. Our principal's breath was pure toxic nuclear waste. It made our eyes water and burned the insides of our noses. My friends and I practically gagged.

"I know you're up to something," Monkey Breath insisted. "You're *always* up to something. Just tell me what it is and we'll get this over with."

"Get what over with?" I asked.

Monkey Breath blinked. With a sudden movement he straightened up, looking alarmed. "Did you hear that?"

"What?" asked Wilson.

"Shhh!" Our principal pressed a finger to his lips. "Listen."

We listened but didn't hear anything.

"What are we listening for?" Dusty asked.

"That!" Monkey Breath gasped.

"What?" I asked.

Monkey Breath's eyes darted left and right. "They're in the walls."

"Who?"

"The little green women."

My friends and I slumped down in our chairs. The little green women were nothing new. Monkey Breath had been mumbling about them for weeks. Sometimes he thought they were outside. Sometimes he thought they were in closets. But they'd never been in the walls before.

"Down on the floor!" our principal cried.

We dove to our hands and knees. Monkey Breath crawled out from behind his desk and through the metal detector to the metal door. He undid the bolt, pushed the door open, and crawled out into the main office.

Not knowing what else to do, my friends and I followed. We kept crawling until we reached a pair of pointy red high-heeled shoes. We looked up. Ms. Fortune was standing over us with a big frown on her face.

Dusty, Wilson, and I jumped to our feet. Meanwhile, Monkey Breath crawled behind the office counter and disappeared through the door to the counseling room.

"Guess you're wondering why we all crawled out of the office, huh?" I asked as I dusted off my knees.

To my surprise, our assistant principal shook her head. "Where were the little green women this time?"

"In the walls," answered Dusty.

Ms. Fortune sighed. Her sighs smelled a lot better than Monkey Breath's. "Yesterday they were under his desk. And the day before that they were in the ceiling."

"Those little green women sure do get around," Wilson cracked.

Ms. Fortune didn't smile. "This is serious, boys. The principal is the captain, and the school is his ship. Right now, this school is in serious danger of sinking."

I think my friends and I were a little surprised that she'd told us that. After all, we were just seventh graders. "You better go back to your classes," she said.

But out in the hall, we paused to reflect on what we'd just heard.

"What do you think happens when a school sinks?" I wondered.

"Maybe the grades go down," guessed Wilson.

Meanwhile, Dusty nodded down the empty hall. "Lunch just ended, dudes."

"So?"

"The teachers' lounge should be empty."

Wilson gave me a nervous look. "What if we get caught?"

"By who?" Dusty asked. "Monkey Breath's crawling around trying to escape from the little green ladies."

Dusty pushed on the teachers' lounge door and went in.

Out in the hall, Wilson and I hesitated. Something weird happens when one of your friends goes through a door. You feel this incredible need to follow. It's almost like it's in the genes. Wilson and I had no choice. We followed.

There aren't a lot of places that really make me nervous. The doctor's office when I know I have to get a shot, the dentist's office . . . and the teachers' lounge. It's *The Totally Forbidden Zone*. You step in there and you've gone way beyond trespassing.

Not that the teachers' lounge *looks* really scary or anything. Inside are a couple of lunch tables, a bunch of chairs, and two ratty-looking couches. A bulletin board on the wall has some ripped-out cartoons and a poster from the teachers' union. Add to that a refrigerator, a microwave, a coffee-maker, and, of course, the soda machine.

The soda machine was one of those older models. Not nearly as flashy as the new ones you see in the supermarket. Dusty had a grin on his face that must have been a mile wide as he pointed at the price.

"Amazing!" I said. "Why do they sell it so cheap?"

"It must be a special deal for teachers only," said Wilson.

"And for us, too." Dusty shoved his hand into his pocket to get some change.

And that's when the teachers' lounge door started to open.

My friends and I froze. There wasn't time to hide. We were in plain sight in the teachers' lounge and we were about to be busted.

Until we saw the green hair. Cheech the Leech stuck his head in. "I thought I heard your voices!"

Wilson rolled his eyes and put his hands over his heart as if he'd almost had a heart attack. Even Dusty looked a little bug-eyed.

"Geez, dude, you totally freaked us," I said.

"Oh, you mean by coming in here?" Cheech realized. "What are you guys doing in here anyway?"

"Leaving," I said.

Dusty didn't argue. He was too freaked. We all went back out to the hall. Cheech stared at us in wonder. I guess I better tell you a little bit about him. He's one of those guys who follows the cool kids and imitates whatever they do. My friends and I used to give him a hard time about that, but then we changed. The truth is, Cheech is an okay kid.

"What were you doing in there?" he asked.

"Uh, nothing," said Dusty. We weren't at the point where we were ready to share our secrets with him.

"Come on, tell me," said Cheech. "I thought you guys were gonna be my friends."

"We are, Cheech," Dusty said. "We consider you a bud, but you're not inner circle yet."

"How do I get to be inner circle?" Cheech asked.

"It takes time," I answered.

"And you have to do something about the hair." Wilson pointed at Cheech's head. "Dude, no one's dyeing their hair green anymore."

Cheech touched his hair self-consciously. "They're not?"

"That's way old," said Dusty.

"You think I should just bleach the top blond?" Cheech asked.

"Dude, you should do whatever *you* want to do," I said. "Don't worry so much about what everyone else is doing."

"That's what you guys do?" Cheech asked.

"Definitely," I said.

"Okay," Cheech said. "That's what I'll do. Can I be inner circle now?"

"No, dude," Dusty said. "We'll tell you when."

**10**

After that, we headed to class. The rest of the day passed normally. Alice was still freaking out about the recycling competition. Gary Gordon was still acting like a jerk. And even though we didn't see Monkey Breath, we could assume he was still being weird about the little green women.

At the end of the day, I was dumping some books in my locker when Dusty and Wilson came by.

"Ready?" Dusty asked.

"For what?" I asked.

Wilson didn't look happy. "Dusty wants to go back into the teachers' lounge."

"Why?" I asked.

"I *told* you guys," Dusty said. "That's where the cheapest sodas in the world are."

"And *I'm* telling you, if we get caught, we are dead meat," I reminded him.

"Don't worry so much," Dusty replied.

One good thing about the teachers at Hard Marks Middle School: They want to get out of school as fast as the kids do. We didn't have to wait long until the teachers' lounge was empty.

Inside the lounge Dusty pulled some coins out of his pocket. He fed them into the soda machine and pushed a button. We heard a clunking sound, and then a bright red can of Coke rolled out of the slot at the bottom.

Dusty popped the top and took a long sip. "Only the best. No cut-rate brands for the hard-working teachers of Hard Marks."

He fed some more coins into the machine and before long, all three of us were enjoying ice-cold caffeinated bubbly.

"You think maybe this is why people become teachers?" Wilson asked.

"Could be," said Dusty. He tilted his head back, drained the can of Coke, and then crushed it in his fist.

And that's when the doorknob started to turn.

My friends and I had forgotten that there actually were two people who liked to stay late at school — those teachers in love, Mr. Gutsy and Ms. Fortune. (Before she became assistant principal, Ms. Fortune was a science teacher.)

Every day after school, the two lovebirds exercised together in the W and E room. And now they'd come to the teachers' lounge to get something cold to drink.

"I'm extremely worried about Chump," said Ms. Fortune as she opened up the refrigerator and pulled out a bottle of water.

"The green women again?" asked Mr. Gutsy as he fed coins into the soda machine.

"It's worse than ever," said Ms. Fortune. "Today he canceled all his appointments and refused to talk to anyone on the phone. You can't run a school that way."

"That's why they have assistant principals," said Mr. Gutsy.

"But there are certain things only the principal can do," argued Ms. Fortune. "And those things aren't getting done."

"Then maybe they'll have to make *you* the principal," said Mr. Gutsy.

Ms. Fortune frowned and shook her head. "That poor man. He's just become unglued."

"Maybe he'll be better tomorrow," said Mr. Gutsy. "Now come on, we better get going."

The lovebirds left the teachers' lounge. Dusty crawled out from under a couch. I came out from the storage closet. Wilson squeezed out of the corner next to the soda machine.

"That was too close," he groaned, wiping some beads of sweat from his forehead.

"Hey, we didn't get caught, right?" Dusty said.

"Let's just get out of here," I said. We left the lounge. It felt good to be back out in the hall where we were safe.

"So how'd you guys like the sodas?" Dusty asked as we walked down the hall.

"They're great," answered Wilson. "I just don't like what we have to go through to get them."

"That won't be a problem," said Dusty. "In fact, tomorrow we'll be enjoying sodas at lunch."

"Are you crazy?" I asked.

"Probably," said Dusty. "But I think we can do it."

"But why?" I asked.

"Simple," Dusty answered. "*No soda* is the biggest rule in school, right?"

"Right."

"But teachers can have as much as they want, and they only have to pay *one third the regular price*," Dusty pointed out.

"It's, like, totally not fair!" Wilson realized.

"Exactly," agreed Dusty. "And it's time we changed that."

"How?" I asked.

"I'll tell you tomorrow," Dusty answered. He and Wilson stopped in the hall.

"School's over," I said. "Aren't you guys going home?"

"We're going to stay here a little while," Dusty said. "I just thought of a project I'd like Wilson to work on."

"Really?" Wilson's eyes sparkled with delight. There was nothing he liked more than building and inventing stuff.

I gave them both a suspicious look. "Why do I feel like I'm being left out?"

"Because," Dusty replied with a smile, "you are."

**12**

I knew I was being set up for something. Wilson, Dusty, and I may have been best friends, but that didn't stop us from goofing with each other. That night at home, it was driving me crazy. I knew Dusty would never tell me what he had planned, but maybe I could get Wilson to talk. I decided to call him.

Wilson has a little sister named Kelsea who thinks she's a fairy princess. When I dialed their number, the answering machine picked up. Next thing I knew, I was listening to Kelsea sing:

> *Twinkle, twinkle, little star,*
> *Leave a number and who you are.*

I was just about to hang up when Wilson got on the phone. "Hello?"

"Hey, Wilson, it's Kyle."

"Yo, Kyle."

"You have to do something about that answering machine," I said.

"Oh, no, what's she put on it now?" Wilson groaned.

I told him it was the "Twinkle, Twinkle, Little Star" song.

"I'll tape over it," Wilson said. "You know what it was last week?"

"No."

"You won't believe it. Hold on, I've got it on another tape right here."

I heard some clicking sounds and then Kelsea started singing to the tune of "The Lion Sleeps Tonight":

> *In this home, this quiet home,*
> *There's no one home tonight.*
> *Leave a message, a simple message,*
> *Make sure your number's right. . . .*

Wilson got back on the phone. "Can you believe I have to live with that?"

"It's bad, dude," I agreed.

"And you guys wonder why I hate single digits," Wilson grumbled. "So I bet you're calling because it's killing you that you don't know what Dusty's planning."

"You got it," I said.

"Sorry, dude, top secret."

"This is no fair," I complained.

"When the time is right, you'll know," Wilson said, and hung up.

# 13

"It's insanity," I said at the bus stop the next morning. We'd gotten to the bus stop early to discuss Dusty's plan.

"It's not insanity," countered Dusty. "It's a challenge."

"It could be challenging insanity," Wilson said.

"Or an insane challenge," added Dusty.

The dwarf pod arrived. The dwarf pod was composed of the Five Dwarfs — Barfy, Sleepy, Burpy, Sneezy, and Farty. They were all little kids and they all wore bright red, yellow, and blue plastic backpacks.

Each morning, the dwarf pod paid us a bus stop tax. This morning, they gave us jaw breakers, bubble gum, and Skittles.

"You're still planning on getting sodas at lunch?" I asked.

"Ever try Skittles and bubble gum at the same time?" Dusty asked as he chewed. "It's not bad."

"Forget about the candy, okay?" I snapped.

"Lunch is the busiest time of day in the teachers' lounge. There is absopositively no way we can get in there without being seen."

"Did I say we wouldn't be seen?" Dusty asked.

"Come on, Dusty," I said. "You're not making sense."

"Okay, here's how we're going to do it," Dusty said. "We are going to volunteer to help Alice win the recycling competition."

"What?" I asked in disbelief.

"You heard me," said Dusty.

I looked at Wilson. "You agreed to this?"

"I got to invent something," Wilson replied sheepishly.

"I don't know what you built," I grumbled, "but I sure hope it makes us invisible."

"You'll see," Dusty said with a big smile.

"**R**eally?!" Alice gasped later in the hall after I told her that my friends and I were going to help with the recycling competition. Alice had a huge smile on her face and a dreamy look in her eyes. I took a step back just in case she tried to do something crazy like throw her arms around my neck and hug me.

"What made you change your mind?" she asked.

I glanced at Dusty.

"He's had a change of heart," Dusty said.

Alice's eyes widened as if she took this to mean more than it did. "And when do you want to start?"

"At lunch," I said.

"With Mr. Recycling Box?" Alice guessed.

"No, with something new." Dusty turned to Wilson. "Please unveil your latest invention."

Wilson went into the metal shop and returned, pushing his newest invention. From the front it looked like a regular bike, but in the back where the rear wheel should have been there was a big green plastic garbage can on two small tricycle wheels.

"Behold the *Trirecycletron*!" Dusty announced.

Wilson stood beside his latest invention and beamed proudly.

"It's perfect!" Alice cried. "You can ride up and down the halls and collect cans and plastic. At the same time, it will remind everyone that they should be recycling!"

"We thought you'd like it," Dusty said, then winked at me.

"And I made it just narrow enough to fit through doorways," added Wilson.

"It's fantastic. I'm so excited!" Alice gushed.

*Briiing!* The homeroom bell rang.

"It's time for Hart TV," Alice said. "Come on, Wilson, we have to go."

Wilson steered the Trirecycletron back into the metal shop and left with Alice. Besides being a mad scientist inventor, he was also the TV techie for Alice's morning show.

Dusty and I started toward homeroom.

"The Trirecycletron," I muttered, shaking my head.

"It's for a worthy cause," said Dusty. "How else

are we going to get cheap sodas from the teachers' lounge?"

"Did it ever occur to you that if you used all
that brainpower for school instead of for scams
you'd probably be in college by now?" I asked.

Dusty made a face. "Who wants to go to college?"

We got into homeroom. Cheech was already
sitting at his desk. His hair was once again its
normal brown color. He gave us a wave. Dusty
and I were sitting down when the TV up in the
corner of the classroom went on. Just like every
other morning, there was Alice sitting alone at
the news desk with her cheerful, fake, news-
anchor smile.

"Good morning. You're watching Hart TV, and
I'm your host, Alice Appleford," she said.

"Doesn't she realize by now that we all know
who she is?" Dusty cracked.

"Maybe she has to remind herself," Cheech
said.

"Good one!" Cheech and I slapped palms.

"And now for some really exciting news," Alice
announced to the greater Hard Marks Middle
School viewing audience. "Our chance to win
the recycling competition and go to Big Splash
got a major boost this morning. One of the most
popular boys in the seventh grade, Kyle Brawly,
is personally going to start a lunchtime program
to increase our recycling efforts. And he hopes

other boys will follow his example. Way to go, Kyle."

The next thing I knew, every kid in homeroom was staring at me with looks that ranged from wonder to sheer disbelief.

**15**

Let me explain. I have nothing against re-cycling. In fact, I'm totally in favor of saving the environment, and the whales, and the giant panda bears, and anything else that needs saving. What I'm against is how everything at Hard Marks gets turned into a competition. I mean, you can't even sneeze without the kid next to you needing to sneeze louder.

When it comes to recycling, I believe that people definitely should recycle . . . because it's the right thing to do, not because they'll win some kind of prize.

Anyway, the reason all the kids in homeroom were staring at me was because they all know how I feel about competition. So for Alice to suddenly announce that I was joining the recycling effort pretty much made me look like one of the world's bigger hypocrites.

\* \* \*

"Aw, look who's here. It's Mr. Recycling Competition." It was after homeroom, and I was out in the hall with Dusty and Cheech. The speaker of those words was none other than Gary "The Geek" Gordon.

"Drop dead, Gary," I said.

"Kiss-up," Gary shot back. "Brownnose. Teachers' pet."

The words burned holes in my ears. Of all the bad things you could call me, those had to be the worst. Dusty must have seen my hands balling into fists because he placed a hand on my shoulder. "Easy, dude. No sense making a bad scene worse."

But Gary saw my fists and made fists of his own.

"Hey, bring it on," he taunted. "I don't see anything I can't handle with one hand tied behind my back."

"You couldn't handle Lisa Simpson with one hand tied behind your back," Cheech said.

Gary's mouth fell open, and a couple of kids around us chuckled. Dusty, Cheech, and I headed off to our next class.

"You know, Cheech," I said, "I never knew you were so quick with the cut-downs. You're pretty funny."

Cheech's face turned red. "Thanks, Kyle."

"It's the kind of talent you should use," Dusty said.

"How?" asked Cheech.

"Well, I don't know," Dusty said. "Sometimes you just have to keep your eyes open for an opportunity."

The words had hardly left his mouth when around the corner came Alice and her friend Rachel Smath. Rachel is this fairly cute girl with red hair and an upturned nose.

When Alice saw me, her eyes brightened. "How'd you like this morning's show?"

I forced a smile onto my face. There was no reason to tell her that thanks to her show I'd been called a kiss-up for the first time in my life. It would be a long time before the word stopped echoing in my head.

"Uh, it was okay," I said.

The smile on Alice's face slowly disappeared. "Just okay?"

"You need a coanchor," Dusty suddenly said.

Alice nodded. "Yes, that's what I've been telling Kyle for weeks."

"Kyle's not your man," Dusty said.

Alice frowned. "Then who is?"

Dusty grinned. "We'll get back to you on that."

Dusty, Cheech, and I continued down the hall toward our next class.

"What was that all about?" I asked.

Dusty put his hand on Cheech's shoulder. "I think I just found a way to put Cheech's talents to work and make Hart TV a little less boring."

# 16

That afternoon, Wilson, Dusty, and I ate lunch quickly and then went to metal shop to get the Trirecycletron. Wilson had built a small footrest on either side of the green garbage can so that Dusty and I could hold on while Wilson pedaled.

Instead of heading for the teachers' lounge, Wilson started riding toward the lower-grade wing.

"Why are we going to the single digits?" I asked as I hung onto the back of the Trirecycletron.

"Gotta make it look real," Dusty explained. "If we just go straight to the teachers' lounge every day, someone might get suspicious."

Wilson had mounted a clown's horn on the front of the Trirecycletron, and he beeped it so that the little kids knew he was coming. I have to admit it was kind of fun, like being in a parade. All the little kids poured out of their classrooms and lined the hall. When they learned we were coming to collect recycling materials, they all hurried back into their rooms to get stuff. The weird thing was, the Trirecycletron may have started as a joke, but it did the job.

After we finished the lower-school wing, we headed to the teachers' lounge. Thanks to the little kids, the garbage can was about half full of cans and plastic bottles.

"This is perfect," Dusty said. "Just perfect!"

"Why?" I asked.

"You'll see."

Wilson stopped the Trirecycletron outside the teachers' lounge and honked the clown horn. Ms. Step, the girls' gym teacher, opened the door. Behind her, about a dozen teachers were sitting at tables eating. They craned their necks to see what the honking was about.

"Trirecycletron, here to recycle," Wilson announced, and pedaled right past Ms. Step and into the lounge with Dusty and me hanging on. Next to the soda machine was a big cardboard recycling box for the empty soda cans. Instead of picking up the box and dumping its contents into the Trirecycletron's garbage can, Dusty started to pick out the empty cans and toss them in one by one.

"So, Kyle," he said loudly, "who do you think's going to win the World Series this year?"

I stared at him like he was crazy.

"Just play along," Dusty whispered under his breath.

So Dusty, Wilson, and I had this ridiculous conversation about baseball while we slowly tossed the cans from the recycling box into the Trirecycletron. After a while, the teachers hardly seemed to notice us.

Finally, the recycling box in the teachers' lounge was empty.

"Okay, guys," Dusty said. "Time to go."

"But — " I started to say that we'd forgotten something. Dusty gave me a sharp look that said he knew what he was doing.

Out in the hall he started to grin. "That was perfect, just perfect!"

"Perfect except for one thing," I said. "We didn't get the sodas."

"We will, dude," he said. "Believe me, we will."

It turned out that Dusty wanted the first visit to the teachers' lounge to be a dry run, just to see how the teachers would react to having us in the lounge with the Trirecycletron. The next day and the day after that, we went back with the Trirecycletron, but Dusty still didn't try to buy a soda. He said we needed time "to practice" and to let the teachers get used to us. But the fourth day was different.

"This is it, dudes," he said as we rode the Trirecycletron toward the teachers' lounge.

"The real thing?" Wilson gasped.

Dusty nodded. "Either we come out with the goods, or we don't come out at all."

Inside the lounge, we parked the Trirecycletron about two feet in front of the soda machine. Dusty and I stood between the Trirecycletron and the machine. Anyone looking in our direction would see the Trirecycletron and us, but not much of the soda machine. And they definitely wouldn't see Wilson crouched behind me, feeding coins into the money slot.

Dusty and I slowly transferred empty soda cans from the recycling box to the Trirecycletron. We talked loudly about baseball. Meanwhile, behind us, Wilson bought three cans of soda. These we also dropped into the Trirecycletron and made sure they were covered by a layer of empty cans.

The mission went precisely as planned. A few moments later, we left the teachers' lounge with the sodas.

"We did it, dudes!" Wilson whispered out in the hall.

"Success!" Dusty held up his fist.

"That made me thirsty," I said in a low voice. "Let's drink!"

"Right," agreed Wilson as he got back on the Trirecycletron and started to pedal. "Now that we've got the sodas."

"The whole idea is to drink them," said Dusty.

Wilson stopped pedaling. The Trirecycletron slowly rolled to a halt in the empty hall. My friends and I looked at one another with puzzled expressions on our faces.

We'd succeeded in our most daring mission ever!

We'd scored the world's cheapest sodas from the teachers' lounge!

It was time to enjoy the fruits of our victory!

The problem was, where?

# 18

"We could drink them in the bathroom," Wilson suggested.

Dusty winced. "The whole idea was to have soda with lunch. You want to eat lunch in the boys' room?"

"Barf-o-rama, dudes," I groaned.

"But we can't eat in the cafeteria, either," Wilson said. "If anyone sees us with sodas, they're gonna want to know where we got them."

"Plus, we're not supposed to have them anyway," I pointed out.

"I know!" Dusty cried. "The media center! We can get a table in the back where no one will see."

Mr. Hush, the librarian, lets kids eat in the media center if they promise to study and stay quiet. They also have to promise they'll be neat and clean up any messes. We left the Tri-recycletron outside the media center and went back to the cafeteria to get our lunches.

By the time we got to the cafeteria, the lunch line was pretty short. My friends and I got on line and came out of the kitchen with trays in no time. We were just starting out of the cafeteria when someone called, "Dudes! Wait up!"

It was Cheech.

"Listen, Dusty," Cheech said. "I've been thinking about what you said. You're right. I'd be perfect as Alice's coanchor on Hart TV."

"What?" Wilson asked. He hadn't heard about Dusty's idea yet.

"Uh, yeah, great," Dusty stammered. "Glad you agree. We'll have to talk about it later."

"Why can't we talk about it now?" Cheech asked.

"We just can't," said Dusty.

"Why not?" asked Cheech.

"We're gonna go eat lunch in the media center and study," I said.

"Cool, I'll come with you," Cheech said.

My friends and I shared a look. It wasn't that we didn't want Cheech to come with us. We just didn't want him to know about the sodas.

"It would be better if you didn't," Wilson said.

Cheech began to pout. "Oh . . . because I'm not in the inner circle?"

Now we felt bad. No one wanted to hurt Cheech's feelings.

"It's not that," I said. "We really have some serious studying to do."

"Don't I know it, dudes," said Cheech. "The big test on the Civil War is this afternoon."

"It is?" Wilson asked.

"Oh, my gosh!" I realized. "He's right!"

Cheech looked puzzled. "Isn't that what you guys were talking about?"

Wilson, Dusty, and I shared sheepish looks. The truth was, we'd all forgotten about that test. Now we were *really* stuck.

"You know much about the Civil War?" Dusty asked Cheech.

"Tons," said Cheech. "You want me to help you guys study? Great! We'd better get going. There isn't much time, and we've got a lot of material to cover."

We had no choice but to let him come to the media center with us.

**19**

All the way to the media center, Cheech talked about becoming Alice's coanchor. "I've got it all planned, dudes. I'll be the wise guy, and Alice will be my straight man. It'll be a blast! She'll talk about the serious stuff, and I'll crack jokes. That way kids'll find out what's going on, but at the same time they'll be entertained."

"Sounds, er, great," Dusty said. You could see he wasn't really listening. We were still trying to figure out how to get rid of Cheech so we could enjoy our sodas in private.

We turned the corner. Down the hall, the Trirecycletron was still parked outside the media center. My friends and I shared hopeless glances. We stopped outside the media center doors.

Cheech frowned. "Aren't we going in?"

"In a moment," Dusty answered, and shoved his hand into the garbage can behind the Trirecycletron. He reached through the cans and pulled one out. Cheech frowned, but then he must have seen what the rest of us saw: Unlike the empty cans, this one was covered with a film of tiny drops of condensation. Cheech reached forward and touched it. His eyes went wide.

"It's cold!" he gasped.

He watched in wonder as Dusty dug through the cans and pulled out the other two sodas.

"You have any more?" Cheech asked.

Dusty shook his head. "Sorry, dude, three's all we got."

Cheech's face fell and he nodded as if he understood. "I guess it's because I'm still not in the inner circle. So where'd you get them anyway?"

"The teachers' lounge," Dusty said.

Cheech's jaw dropped. "For real?"

I have to admit that it was kind of fun to watch how Cheech reacted to our newest scam. You would have thought we'd told him that we'd just broken into Fort Knox and gotten away with all the gold.

In the media center, we took a table way in the back. We propped up our books and opened them, then put the cans inside. Dusty had planned it so well he even brought straws. If anyone looked at us, they would have seen kids with their faces in books. Little would they suspect that behind those books we were sipping sodas.

In the meantime, Cheech tutored us on what he thought might be on the Civil War test. I was kind of impressed by how much he knew. Also, he didn't ask to share our sodas or anything gross like that. And he didn't say much about being Alice's coanchor, either. All he asked was if tomorrow we could get him a soda, too.

# 20

The next day when we returned to the teachers' lounge, we had to buy four sodas. One for each of us and the fourth for Cheech.

"Know what's amazing?" Wilson said as we left the lounge and headed toward the media center on the Trirecycletron. "We just bought *four* sodas for about the same amount of money as we'd spend for *one* at the cineplex."

"They rip you off at the cineplex," I said.

"Interesting," said Dusty.

"What's so interesting about it?" I asked.

"Let me ask you a question," Dusty said. "How good a friend is Cheech?"

"What do you mean?" I asked.

"Well, is he a good enough friend that we'll share teachers' lounge sodas with him?" Dusty asked.

"Duh, looks like it," I said. After all, we'd just bought an extra soda for him.

"But is he a good enough friend that we'll share the savings, too?" asked Dusty.

"Oh, I get it," Wilson realized. "You want to charge him a little more. That way he'll help pay for our sodas!"

"Exactly," said Dusty. "If we just charge him what a soda *normally* costs. And I mean, not what those thieves at the cineplex charge, but just what a soda costs at the store. Then he'll be happy to have a soda in school, and we'll get sodas for practically nothing."

"And then the next thing you know, we'll open our own store, right here in the school!" I joked. "We'll be richer than Bill Gates!"

Once again, we left the Trirecycletron in the hall outside the media center. Inside, Cheech was waiting for us at one of the tables in the back. He had a hopeful look on his face, as if he was praying we'd remembered to get him a soda.

I made a circle with my thumb and index finger. A big smile appeared on Cheech's face.

"This is *beyond* way cool, dudes!" he said when we sat down and passed him his soda.

"Shhh!" Dusty pressed a finger to his lips and nodded over at Mr. Hush, who was watching us.

"Don't forget," I whispered as I hid my soda behind my book. "We're here for *serious* studying."

"So what are we going to study today?" Wilson asked.

"I don't know," I said. "Do we have any tests this afternoon?"

"No," answered Cheech.

"Well, we better do something," said Wilson.

"Let's have less talking and more studying," Mr. Hush called from the checkout desk.

My friends and I pressed our faces into our books and tried to find something to study while we enjoyed our lunch and sodas. Mr. Hush spent the whole lunch period watching us. By the time we finished our sodas and lunches, the period was almost over.

"I hate to say this," Dusty said in a low voice as we got up to take our trays back to the cafeteria, "but at this rate, we may actually learn something!"

**21**

As you probably know, there's no such thing as a secret in middle school. We didn't say anything to anyone. But two days later I came out of the lunch line with my tray and found my good friend Melody Autumn Sunshine waiting for me.

"Hey, handsome, where're you going?" she asked.

"The media center," I answered.

Melody gave me a questioning look. "You? Since when?"

By now, Dusty, Wilson, and Cheech had come out of the kitchen with their trays.

"You're *all* going to the media center?" Melody raised a suspicious eyebrow.

I looked at my friends. There was no way I could ever lie to her. "We have to tell her, guys."

We told her. The thing about Melody is her parents were hippies back in the old days and they still have a lot of hippie ideas. Melody wears these funny Indian-print dresses to school, and she braids her long brown hair and always wears beads and lots of silver rings on her fingers and toes. Melody's parents are into eating healthy, so you'd figure maybe Melody would be that way, too. But you'd be wrong. She is a big-time junk food junkie.

A little while later, Mr. Hush looked shocked as all five of us paraded past him and into the media center. At our table in the back, we sat down and propped up our books with our cans of soda behind them. Our daily lunchtime study group had officially expanded to five.

# 22

For the next few days, our "study group" spent each lunch period in the media center. But each day, Dusty seemed to spend less and less time with us.

"Be back in a second," he'd say, then get up. Melody, Cheech, and I would watch quietly as Dusty left the media center.

"Am I the only one who's noticed that this is the fourth day in a row Dusty's gobbled down lunch and left?" I finally whispered.

Wilson looked up from his book and blinked. "Huh?"

"Looks like Wilson's answer is yes." Melody winked. "But I've noticed."

"Me, too," said Cheech.

"Where do you think he's going?" I whispered.

"Why don't you follow him and find out?" she said.

"All right, I will."

I got up and left the media center. The first

thing I noticed was that the Trirecycletron was missing. I started down the hall. I had the feeling that wherever I found the Trirecycletron was where I'd find Dusty, too.

The Trirecycletron was parked outside the boys' room. I was just about to go in when two sixth graders squeezed past me and went in first.

"You sure this is the place?" one asked as he pushed open the bathroom door.

"That's what Jimmy said," answered the second.

The two sixth graders went in. I followed. Inside the bathroom they went down to the last stall and knocked on the closed stall door.

"Password?" a voice said from inside the stall.

"Jimmy sent us," one of the sixth graders answered.

"How many?" asked the voice inside the stall.

"Two." One of the sixth graders knelt down and slid some money under the stall door. Two cans of Coke came sliding out.

"Don't get caught drinking them," the voice inside the stall warned.

"Right. Thanks!" The sixth graders hid the cans in their backpacks and hurried out.

I went down to the stall door and knocked.

"Password?" the voice inside said.

"How about 'Dusty Lane is going to get his butt in a sling when Monkey Breath finds out he's selling sodas in the boys' room'?" I asked.

The stall door opened. Inside, Dusty had half a dozen cans of Coke stacked neatly on the toilet cover.

"You are unbelievable," I groaned.

"Thank you," Dusty said with a smile.

"You know what's gonna happen when — "

"It's not going to happen," Dusty cut me short.

"Get real," I said. "Kids are going to be drinking sodas all over school, and no one's going to notice?"

"I remind everyone to be careful and not get caught."

"Like they're all going to listen," I said in disbelief.

"Hopefully," Dusty said. "If they want to keep getting sodas they will."

"Come on, dude," I said. "Do *you* listen when someone tells you not to do something?"

"Well . . . " Dusty didn't exactly answer.

"See?" I said.

"Do you know how much money I'm making?" Dusty asked. "I sell each can for twice what I pay for it, and the kids *still* feel like they're getting a great deal."

The bathroom door opened, and three sixth graders came in.

"Where's the guy with the sodas?" one asked.

"Right here," Dusty replied with a smile. "At your service."

# 23

Dusty would not be stopped. Instead, he expanded the business! He found a girl named Claire to sell sodas out of the girls' room for him. It got to the point where we hardly even saw Dusty at lunch anymore. He'd assigned Cheech to go with Wilson and me on the Trirecycletron to the teachers' lounge and buy sodas. We'd take our sodas to the library and Dusty would take the Trirecycletron (and a bunch of full cans) to the boys' room.

"Why is Dusty doing this?" I asked Wilson one day at lunch. We were sitting at our regular table in the library. Dusty wasn't there, of course. He was in the boys' room becoming the Bill Gates of soda pop.

"Doing what?" Wilson asked as he licked ketchup off a french fry.

"Risking everything just to sell soda," I said.

"For the money," Wilson said. "You should see the CD burner he just bought."

I shook my head. "I don't believe that. Maybe Dusty's buying stuff with the money he makes, but that's not why he's doing it. He doesn't care about money that much. There has to be another reason."

"Ask him," Wilson said with a shrug.

"I will," I said.

After lunch we ran into Dusty in the hall.

"So how's business?" I asked him.

"Great," Dusty said. "Check this out." He opened his backpack and took out a brand-new MP-3 player. "Top of the line, dude. The best money can buy."

"Dude, tell me the truth," I said. "Why are you *really* doing this?"

Dusty started to point at the MP-3 player, but I stopped him. "No, Dusty. I know you. There's more to this than just buying stuff."

Dusty nodded. "You're right, Kyle. I think it's time we changed our philosophy. Instead of going where no rule has gone before, I think we have to start *changing* the rules. And the first one I want to change is *No Soda*."

"What's your plan?" I asked.

"To take this scam to the point where *every single kid* in school is drinking soda at lunch," Dusty explained. "Then we can tell Monkey Breath to change the rule and we'll have *the whole school* behind us."

"But what if Monkey Breath catches you before that?" I asked.

"The scam won't work," Dusty admitted. "But he's not going to catch me. In the last two weeks, we've doubled our sales. Everything's going great."

"What about that?" Wilson asked, pointing at a soda can sitting on the window ledge.

Dusty's eyes widened with surprise. He went over to the window, grabbed the soda can, and stuck it in his backpack. "I'm gonna have to remind the kids again," he grumbled. "If they don't stop leaving empty cans around, we're gonna get busted bad."

The trouble with kids is no matter how many times you remind them, they still forget. The more sodas Dusty sold, the more cans seemed to get left around. We started finding them on the library bookshelves, and inside desks, and under bushes outside. Between selling sodas and picking up the ones kids left behind, Dusty hardly had any time left for school.

"I don't get it," he muttered one afternoon at his locker as we got ready to leave school. "I keep telling everyone that if they're not careful with their cans we're gonna get caught. And if we get caught, they're not gonna get any more sodas. Sounds pretty simple, right?"

"Maybe you'll have to start paying for returns like they do at the store," Wilson joked.

"Better yet, why not cut Monkey Breath into

the deal?" I teased. "Then you won't *ever* have to worry about being caught."

"Talk about Monkey Breath," Wilson whispered, and nodded down the hall. Our principal was walking toward us with a soda can in his hand and a major frown on his face.

Monkey Breath's black suit was ripped at the knees and elbows from crawling on the floor. His hair stuck out in all directions like it was full of static electricity. His eyes twitched and his chin was covered with dark stubble. As he walked, he would suddenly twist around and look behind him as if he thought he was being followed.

He came up to us and held out the soda can. "Boys, do you know what this is?"

"Uh, looks like a soda can," I said.

"It's the third one I've found today," he said. "I don't understand it. Students are strictly forbidden to bring soda into school. And the teachers know not to take their cans out of the teachers' lounge. The only thing I can think of is — "

"The little green ladies!" Dusty gasped.

"Where?" Monkey Breath spun around. He raised his hands to karate position as if ready to fight.

"Nowhere," said Dusty.

Monkey Breath frowned and lowered his hands. "But you just said . . . "

"He meant that they could be the ones behind the soda cans," said Wilson.

Monkey Breath's eyebrows rose. "You think?"

"Wouldn't surprise me," said Dusty. "Right, guys?"

"Right," said Wilson.

"Oh, yeah, without a doubt." I nodded.

Monkey Breath frowned for a moment. Then he made a fist and crushed the empty soda can. "It's them, all right! Little green women with soda cans. I knew it!"

He stormed off down the hall, muttering to himself.

"It's, like, he totally forgot we were here," I said.

"That," Wilson said, "is one sick puppy."

## 24

The next day Dusty added a ten-cents-a-can surcharge to the price of a soda. Kids protested the price increase until he explained that all they had to do was return the empty can and they'd get their dime back.

At lunchtime, Wilson and I visited the boys' room to see how the new system was working. As soon as the boys' room door closed behind us, we found ourselves in a line.

"What is this?" Wilson asked.

"The line to buy sodas," a kid in front of him answered.

"No, it's not," said the kid in front of that kid. "This is the line to return cans. The line to buy sodas is over there."

Now we noticed a second line. On one stall door was a handwritten sign that said SALES. On the stall next to it was a sign that said RETURNS.

Dusty was inside the SALES stall, selling sodas.

Cheech was in the RETURNS stall, taking the empty cans back.

Wilson and I went over to the SALES stall.

"Hey, no cutting!" a kid in line yelled.

"We're not cutting," I said. "This is just a sales call."

Inside the SALES stall, Dusty was selling sodas as fast as he could. Beads of sweat clung to his forehead.

"Business looks good," Wilson observed.

"Sure is," Dusty said.

I poked my head into the RETURNS stall where Cheech was busy exchanging dimes for empty cans. The floor of the stall and the toilet cover were overflowing with cans.

*Briiinggg!* Outside in the hall the bell rang. It was time to change classes. In no time the boys' room emptied out. Dusty came out of the SALES stall with a wad of bills that he stuffed into his pocket.

"Man, this has to be the best day yet," he said with a big smile.

"We better get to class," said Cheech.

He and Cheech started out of the boys' room.

"Uh, guys?" I said.

Dusty stopped and looked back. "Yeah?"

I pointed at all the cans on the floor of the RETURNS stall. "Aren't you forgetting something?"

Dusty and Cheech stared at the cans on the floor and then at each other.

"What do we do?" Cheech asked.

Dusty had to think fast. Monkey Breath was constantly coming into the boys' room to check for troublemakers. He was bound to see the cans. He might assume they were left by the little green women. Then again, he might not.

"Anyone know where there's some empty lockers?" Dusty asked.

"There's one near mine," said Wilson.

Dusty put down his backpack and unzipped it. "Okay, guys, start loading."

By pulling out a lot of books we were able to get almost all of the cans into our backpacks. They rattled as we pulled the backpacks on and left the boys' room, carrying our books in our arms.

"Hold it," someone said.

My friends and I froze. Coming up the hall toward us was Ms. Fortune.

## 25

You could tell by the way Ms. Fortune was looking at us that something was bothering her.

"Shouldn't you boys be in class?" she asked.

"That's where we're going right now," Dusty answered.

Ms. Fortune nodded, but she put her hands on her hips and scowled at us, as if she knew something wasn't right and just couldn't quite figure out what it was.

"Uh, is something wrong?" I asked innocently.

The lines in her forehead deepened. Then she shook her head. "Just go to class, boys."

My friends and I started to take off down the hall, but as soon as we did, the cans in our backpacks started to rattle. We instantly slowed down and looked back over our shoulders to see if Ms. Fortune had noticed.

"That's good, boys," she said with an approving nod. "Walk, don't run."

My friends and I walked slowly, careful not to make the cans in our backpacks rattle.

"That was close," Wilson gasped.

"Believe it," I said. "She knew we were up to something."

"How?" Cheech asked.

"The books," Dusty said. "Here we are walking around with full backpacks, but at the same time we've got books in our arms."

"And nobody in school carries *that* many books," added Wilson.

"So let's make this fast before she figures it out," Dusty said.

Wilson led us to the empty locker near his own. It had no lock and inside were some loose papers and an old tennis shoe. We quickly unzipped our backpacks and started to stuff all the cans in. The cans banged around inside the metal locker.

"Not so loud!" Dusty hissed.

"You can have fast or you can have quiet," I said. "But you can't have fast *and* quiet."

"Okay, okay, let's just get it done," Dusty grunted. A second later the cans were all in the locker. Dusty slammed the locker door closed. He had the biggest grin on his face. "Dudes, we'll wait until we've filled up every empty locker around. Then we'll bag all the cans and take them over to the Super Stop & Shop. Not only will I make money selling the sodas, I'll get all that *'returns'* money, too! This scam is golden."

**26**

The scam went another week without a hitch. Dusty was buying tons of sodas in the teachers' lounge and reselling them like crazy in the boys' room. Wilson and I no longer rode the Trirecycletron. Dusty now had his own crew of kids to do that.

One day at lunchtime, Wilson and I were going down the hall toward the cafeteria when we noticed Monkey Breath standing in the school lobby. Our principal was staring through the glass front doors at a big soda truck parked in front of the school. Three men in gray uniforms were loading cases of soda onto hand trucks and wheeling them toward the doors.

Inside, they headed down the hall to the teachers' lounge. Monkey Breath scratched his head.

Wilson and I shared a knowing look. Dusty might have thought his scam was golden last week, but this week we could tell that trouble was coming.

Dusty must have known it, too. Because he and Cheech showed up in the cafeteria toward the end of lunch looking seriously worried.

"You know about Monkey Breath?" I asked.

"What about him?" Dusty asked.

Wilson and I described seeing our principal watching the soda guys making their delivery that morning.

"We have a different problem," Dusty said.

"What's wrong?" I couldn't help teasing. "You need help counting all your money?"

"No, dudes," Dusty replied. "We've run out of places to stash empty cans. You know any more empty lockers?"

Wilson and I shook our heads. By now we'd told him about every single empty locker we knew.

"What about the empty gym lockers?" Wilson asked.

"Filled them all days ago," Cheech reported. "Come on, guys, think. There's got to be some-place *else* to put empty cans."

Wilson and I thought. Suddenly, Wilson blinked and looked past me. "I think I know the answer, dudes. And here she comes."

I turned around. Alice was headed for our table. She had a big frown on her face and she looked really upset.

**27**

"**K**yle Brawly, I am soooo disappointed in you!" Alice cried. "You promised to help with the recycling competition and you haven't done a thing!"

"I helped with the Trirecycletron," I pointed out.

"But you stopped," Alice said. "And now the Trirecycletron doesn't even go to the lower-grade wing anymore."

"But I, uh — " I started to stammer.

"Don't give me any excuses," Alice yelled. "You can tell the whole school how it's your fault when we lose the recycling competition to Jeffersonville."

"How do you know we're going to lose?" Wilson asked.

"Because my spies tell me Jeffersonville has collected more cans, bottles, and newspapers than we have," Alice reported. "They're going to win the competition and go to Big Splash. Now what are you going to do about it?"

I had to think fast. "Cheech," I said.

"What?" Cheech asked.

"You're the answer," I said.

"Me?" He frowned.

"The answer to what?" Alice asked.

"Cheech, tell her your plan for cohosting the morning TV show," I said.

"But — " Alice started to protest.

"You'll be my straight man," Cheech said.

"Huh?" Alice looked at him like he was crazy.

"This is the answer to all your problems," I said. "Just listen to him, Alice."

"What the morning show needs is comedy," Cheech told her. "It needs laughs, Alice."

"But what about all the announcements?" Alice asked.

"We can do them," Cheech said. "But we'll make it funny, too. Look, let me explain."

Cheech led Alice away, busy explaining his ideas for improving the morning TV show. Alice looked back at me as if she wanted to keep talking about recycling, but Cheech wouldn't let her go.

"You bought some time, dude," Wilson said to me. "But I'm not sure how much."

That's when I had a stroke of pure genius. I turned to Dusty. "There's the answer to all your problems, dude. You've got too many cans, right? Just give them to the recycling competition."

To my total surprise, Dusty shook his head. "No way! Do you know how much money I'll lose?"

"What are you talking about?" Wilson asked. "You're not *losing* money. You're *making* it."

"I'll make a whole lot *more* when I take all those cans over to the Stop & Shop and recycle them myself," Dusty said.

"But I thought this scam wasn't about the money," I reminded him. "I thought it was about changing the *No Soda* rule."

"It is," Dusty insisted. "But, er, it's *also* about the money. Besides, since when do you want to help Alice win the competition? I thought you were against all that competitive stuff."

"I am," I said. "It's just that — "

"Just what?" Dusty demanded.

"Well, it was *your* idea that I volunteer to help recycle," I pointed out. "Remember? That was the whole idea behind the Trirecycletron and getting into the teachers' lounge in the first place."

"Right." Dusty smirked. "So now you're going to try and blame it all on me?"

"I'm not blaming you," I said. "I'm just saying that Alice wouldn't be mad at me if it wasn't for you."

"Hey, here's an idea," Wilson said to Dusty. "Suppose you give *half* your cans to Alice and return the other half to the store?"

But Dusty shook his head. "No way, dude. Every single one of those cans is *mine*. I'm not giving them to anyone for any reason, understand?"

## 28

"I hate to say it, but I'm kind of surprised at Dusty," Wilson said as he and I walked to math class after lunch. "I thought the idea of splitting up all the cans was pretty darn fair."

"Me, too." I nodded.

"I mean, he never could have started this scam if you hadn't agreed to join the recycling competition and I hadn't built the Trirecycletron."

"Believe it," I said.

"I just don't get it," Wilson said. "Why's he being so greedy?"

"It's the money, Wilson," I said. "Dusty's under a money spell."

"But he's never done anything like this before," Wilson said.

"What about the bus stop tax?" I asked.

Wilson's eyes widened a little. "Gee, I never thought of that."

Wilson and I went into math class.

"So what are we going to do?" he asked.

"I don't know," I said. "But Dusty's our friend, and we have to help him through this."

We didn't see Dusty again for the rest of the day, but I had a feeling it wouldn't be hard to find him. All I'd have to do would be to go to the boys' room.

At the end of the day, Wilson and I were at our lockers getting ready to go home when Dusty showed up.

"Whoa, look who's here," Wilson said.

"So what can we do for you, stranger?" I asked.

"I've got a problem, guys," Dusty said.

"*Still* don't know what to do with all your money?" Wilson guessed.

"Seriously, dudes," Dusty said. "I've searched everywhere. There's no place left in school to hide cans. We have no choice. We have to get the cans out of the school."

Wilson turned to me with a fake puzzled expression on his face. "We? Did he say *we* have no choice?"

"Haven't we been in this together from the start?" Dusty asked. "Don't we always share?"

"Well, I don't know, Dusty," Wilson said. "I haven't seen you share any money. The only thing you seem to want to share is *the work*."

Dusty narrowed his eyes. "Okay, okay. Maybe you guys are right. Tell you what. You help me get the cans out of school and you'll get half the refund from the Super Stop & Shop."

Wilson and I gave each other questioning looks.

"That's fair," Wilson said.

"No," I said.

"No, what?" asked Wilson.

"I won't do it for the money," I said. "It'll be for the challenge of sneaking all those cans past Monkey Breath."

"Right!" Dusty said. "That's the spirit! We get all the cans out of school, right under Monkey Breath's nose."

"Right," I said. "And if we're successful, Wilson and I get to keep *all* the refund money."

"But that's not fair!" Dusty gasped.

"You want to get those cans out?" I asked. "Or you want Monkey Breath to find them?"

That's when Wilson turned and said, "Speak of the devil!"

# 29

It was Monkey Breath. His black suit was literally in tatters, hanging in shreds from his body. His white shirt showed through the rips in his jacket. In one hand, he carried a yardstick. In the other hand was an eraser.

"Where are they?" he demanded.

"Who?" Wilson asked.

"The green ladies, dummy," said Dusty.

"Where?" Monkey Breath gasped, and looked around.

"Nowhere," said Dusty.

"Huh?" Monkey Breath looked confused.

"Forget it," Wilson said.

Monkey Breath blinked and stared at us as if he were seeing us for the first time. "What are you boys doing here?"

"We go to school here," I said.

"School has officially ended," Monkey Breath announced.

"And we're about to officially go home," said Wilson.

"Good." Monkey Breath nodded. "I want the halls clear, so when those little green women show up I'll be ready."

Our principal stomped off, peeking into classrooms and even looking in desks, as if little green women might be inside.

Dusty, Wilson, and I left school and started to walk home.

"So how do you plan to get the cans out with Monkey Breath patrolling the halls twenty-four/seven looking for little green women?" I asked Dusty.

Dusty rubbed his chin. "Man, what a bummer. Even if we were here at three in the morning he might still be around. What are we gonna do, guys?"

Wilson tugged at his earlobe. I scratched my head. Dusty's shoulders slumped.

"Man, I can't believe it. This has got to be the greatest scam of my life, and it's all going to come to an end because our psycho principal is convinced he's surrounded by little green women."

"That's it!" Wilson cried.

"What's it?" Dusty asked.

"The answer to how we'll get the cans out of school," said Wilson.

"How?" I asked.

"By giving Monkey Breath exactly what he wants," said Wilson.

Dusty and I shared a frown and then looked back at our friend.

"What does he want?" I asked.

"Little green women, dudes," said Wilson. "What else?"

**30**

Wilson's plan was pure genius. Of course, we'd come to expect that from him. The idea was to create a distraction, something that would keep Monkey Breath busy while we smuggled all the cans out of the school.

"Oh, man, Monkey Breath'll freak," Dusty exclaimed happily the next morning as our bus pulled into the bus circle. "He'll go berserk! He'll be so nuts he won't even notice us!"

All of us grinned. I had to admit that it was the *way* coolest plan we'd ever come up with. Grandma, the old lady who drove our bus, parked and we all got out and joined the crowd of kids heading for the middle-school entrance.

"Kyle Brawly," a voice suddenly growled. It was Alice, and she was fighting through the crowd toward me with narrowed eyes and her hands balled into fists.

I looked left and right for a quick escape.

"Don't you dare try to run away." Alice

planted herself in my path and crossed her arms. "So?"

"So . . . what?" I asked.

"So what are you going to do to save this school from a humiliating defeat?" Alice asked. "What are you going to say when everyone finds out *you're* the reason we're not getting a free school trip to Big Splash?"

"Uh, catch you later, Kyle," Wilson said.

"Yeah, Kyle, be cool," said Dusty.

My friends quickly disappeared into the crowd heading for school.

"So?" Alice said again.

"So . . . uh . . . How'd you like Cheech's idea about cohosting the morning show?" I asked.

"Don't try to change the subject," Alice said. "That might have worked yesterday, but it's not going to work today."

I shrugged. "Okay, Alice, you win. What do you want me to do?"

"I want you to find a way for us to win!" Alice cried. "The competition ends tomorrow at five P.M., and we're definitely behind Jeffersonville."

"Maybe you just have to accept the fact that we can't always win every single time," I said.

Alice narrowed her eyes and glared at me as if I'd just said the absolute worst thing ever.

"Only a loser would say that," she snarled, then stomped away.

# 31

I headed into school. Wilson and Dusty were
waiting just inside the doors.

"What'd she say?" Wilson asked.

"That I'm a loser," I said.

Dusty shook his head. "She's a jerk."

"I know," I said. "It's just that she says she's
going to tell the whole school that it's my fault if
we lose to Jeffersonville."

"Don't sweat it," said Dusty. "All you have to
do is tell them it's not true. Who do you think
they'll believe? You or her?"

I shrugged.

"Look, we have something way more important to discuss," Wilson said. "My plan."

"He's right," said Dusty as we went down the
hall. "Where are we going to find a little green
woman?"

Each of us started to look at the other.

"Hey, don't look at me," I said. "I already had

to dress up as a lunch lady this year. I have more than paid my dues."

We looked at Dusty. "Don't look at me. I'm the only one who knows where all the cans are stashed. I'll be too busy getting them out of school."

We looked at Wilson. "No way, just forget it. I came up with the Trirecycletron. And before that the chair gliders, the Decrustifyer, and the mouseapult."

"But it's *your* plan," Dusty said to him. "If you don't do this, it's not going to work."

"And there's no one else who can do it," I added.

Just then we heard someone say, "Hey, dudes, what's up?" It was Cheech and he was coming toward us.

My friends and I shared a knowing look. We all smiled.

"Good to see you, Cheech," said Dusty.

"Your timing is perfect," added Wilson.

"Timing for what?" Cheech asked.

Dusty put his arm around Cheech's shoulders. "Cheech, my man, this is your lucky day. How'd you like to finally get a chance to join the inner circle?"

## 32

That night I dialed Wilson's phone number. The answering machine picked up, and I listened to Wilson's little sister, Kelsea, sing:

*Telephone, telephone, on the wall,*
*Please tell us who is making this call.*
*Snow White or the dwarfs, it doesn't matter,*
*We'll call you right back for lots of chatter.*

I was just about to hang up when Wilson picked up the phone. "Hello?"

"Have you heard your sister's latest message?" I asked.

"Oh, no," he moaned. "What now?"

"It's from *Snow White and the Seven Dwarfs.*"

"I'll kill her!" Wilson cried.

"Anyway, you talk to Cheech?" I asked.

"Yeah, he says he won't do it," Wilson said. "But I think he's weakening."

"You reminded him that it would mean inner-circle status?" I asked.

"Dusty's even offered him *lifetime* inner-circle status, plus a cut of the daily bus-stop tax, *and* one free soda a day for as long as the scam lasts," Wilson said.

"Wow, he must feel really strongly about this," I said.

"What are we going to do?" Wilson asked.

"I think we have to go ahead with the plan," I said. "Bring everything tomorrow as if Cheech has agreed to be a little green woman."

"But what if he doesn't agree?" Wilson asked.

"Don't think about it," I said.

# 33

"No," Cheech said in homeroom the next morning.

"Don't you want lifetime inner-circle status?" Dusty asked.

"Yes," answered Cheech.

"Don't you want a cut of the daily bus-stop tax?" I asked.

"Absolutely," Cheech replied.

"And you want one free soda a day, right?" said Wilson.

"Of course," said Cheech.

"Then all you have to do is dress up as a little green lady," Dusty said.

Dusty crossed his arms and shook his head. "No."

"Why not?"

"I just can't," Cheech said.

Dusty gave me an unhappy look.

"Hey, don't look at me," I said. "You're the one who needs to keep your business empire going."

Dusty kept working on Cheech all morning. In the hall, in class, every chance he got.

"You know, I have to admit I'm impressed," Wilson said at one point.

"With how hard Dusty's working on Cheech?" I guessed.

"No, with how firm Cheech is being in refusing," Wilson said.

"Good point," I admitted. "Who would have thought Cheech could say no so many times and stick to it?"

It was really starting to look like this was one argument Dusty wasn't going to win. But then we got to lunch.

Wilson and I were sitting at our regular table, watching Alice's last attempt to get kids to recycle. She was standing in front of the garbage cans, and every time someone came by with something that could be recycled, she'd insist they put it in Mr. Recycling Box.

"You have to hand it to Alice," Wilson said. "She never gives up."

"It's still hard to imagine she's gonna get enough bottles and plastic that way to beat Jeffersonville," I said.

Just then Dusty and Cheech came out of the lunch line with trays.

"What are you guys doing here?" I asked as they sat down with us.

"How come you're not running the great soda empire?" asked Wilson.

"The great soda empire is shut down because there's no place left to stash empty cans," Dusty moped. "And with Monkey Breath running around twenty-four/seven I can't get them out of school. Of course, if Cheech here would just relax and cooperate, everything would be fine."

"Aw, come on, Dusty," Cheech complained. "That's not fair."

"Dude, don't you understand that you're our last hope?" Dusty asked. "I mean, I thought you were our friend. A friend wouldn't let another friend down in his hour of need."

"Hour of *greed* is more like it," Wilson said with a wink.

"I'd do it if I could," Cheech said. "I'm serious, man."

"Sorry, dude, but those are just words," Dusty replied. "Anyone can say they're serious about anything, but it doesn't mean a thing if you're not willing to *act* on what you say."

"I'm telling you, man, I'd do *anything*," Cheech insisted.

"Anything *except* dress up as a green woman for about ten lousy minutes," Dusty corrected him. "Even though it would be after school, and there'd be no one around to see."

Cheech winced. For the first time that day, we could see that he was starting to have doubts and was unsure of what to do. Dusty must have been waiting for that because he instantly looked over at the lunch table where Melody was sitting and gave her a quick nod.

Melody got up and came over. At the same moment, Dusty turned to Wilson and me. "Come on, guys, let's take a walk."

"But we're in the middle of lunch," Wilson protested.

"It won't be that long," Dusty said.

Wilson and I got up.

"Hey!" Cheech gasped. "Where're you guys going?"

"Cheech, can I talk to you for a second?" Melody asked as she sat down.

Cheech blinked. Melody was just about the prettiest, smartest, and most popular girl in our grade. If she wanted to talk to him, he wasn't going anywhere.

Meanwhile, Dusty, Wilson, and I took a stroll around the cafeteria. Every time we looked back at our table, Melody was sitting there deep in conversation with Cheech.

"Looks like you had a plan," Wilson said to Dusty.

"Looks like it." Dusty grinned.

"What'd you have to promise Melody to make it happen?" I asked.

Dusty gave me a sly smile. "Believe me, whatever it was, it was worth it."

# 34

Cheech may have been able to refuse Dusty, but he couldn't refuse Melody. Finally, he agreed to Dusty's terms. For exactly ten minutes after school, he would be a green woman.

For the rest of the day, we focused on Dusty's scheme. I'm still not sure why Wilson and I were so into it. I don't think we cared about the money Dusty was offering us as much as we just liked the idea of getting all those cans out of school right under Monkey Breath's nose.

Wilson had brought in a green dress to school, and Melody had a wig and makeup. As soon as school ended, Dusty bolted out of class and headed for the bus circle.

"What's with him?" Wilson asked me.

"He wants to make sure Cheech doesn't change his mind and try to sneak out," I said.

Sure enough, the next time we saw Cheech and Dusty, Cheech had a real guilty look on his face.

"Guess who was trying to escape," Dusty said.

"Can't say I blame you, dude," I said to Cheech.

Cheech shrugged. "Let's just get it over with, okay?"

The plan was to meet Melody behind the curtains on the stage in the cafeteria. That was the same place where I'd dressed up as a lunch lady the time we got rid of the Lunch Monitors from H.E.L.L.

Dusty, Wilson, and I waited out in the hall while Melody helped Cheech get changed.

Dusty rubbed his hands together gleefully. "Man, this is going to be great."

"*If* it works," I reminded him.

"It's gonna work, dude," Dusty predicted. "I can feel it."

"You can feel it?" I repeated in disbelief. "That's a new one."

No sooner had the words left my mouth than Cheech came out from behind the curtains. He was wearing the wig, makeup, and the green dress. Wilson and I looked at Cheech and then back at Dusty.

"You *still* feel like this is going to work?" Wilson asked.

Dusty grimaced. You could see that this wasn't what he'd expected or hoped for.

"Too late to back out now, guys," he groaned.

# 35

Melody came out from behind the curtain. From the way she was frowning, we could tell that she wasn't happy with the end result, either.

"I'm sorry, Dusty," she apologized. "I gave it my best shot. Sometimes it works and sometimes it doesn't."

The problem was that Cheech didn't look like a little green woman. He looked like a green clown.

"Well, I guess that's it," Cheech said with a shrug. "If it's not going to work, I might as well take this stuff off."

"No!" Dusty cried.

"But he really doesn't look much like a little green lady," Melody said.

"Maybe not close up," said Dusty. "Cheech, back up, will you?"

Cheech backed down the hall a few yards and stopped.

"Still looks like Cheech," I said.

"Green Cheech," added Wilson.

"Clown Cheech," said Melody.

"Move back farther," Dusty said.

Cheech backed up some more.

"Still Green Cheech," I said.

"Farther," said Dusty.

Cheech backed up even farther.

"Farther," said Wilson.

By now, Cheech was almost all the way down the hall.

"Now what do you think?" Dusty asked.

"He almost looks like a little green woman," said Wilson.

"That's because he's so far away," I said. "And he looks green because that's how he's dressed. But he still doesn't look like a lady."

"Maybe not, but we agree that he's green and he's little," said Wilson. "That's two out of three and that's not bad."

"He's sixty-six and two-thirds percent there," said Melody.

"Look," Dusty said impatiently, "he's little and he's green, and that's the best we're gonna get, so let's do it already."

## 36

We told Green Cheech that no matter what happened, he shouldn't let Monkey Breath get close enough to see that he wasn't a little green woman. Green Cheech said that suited him just fine because he didn't want to get caught anyway.

"Okay, now, one last time," Dusty said. "How are you going to accomplish your mission?"

"I'm going to stay way down the hall from the main office," Green Cheech answered. "If and when Monkey Breath comes out of the office, I am to call out, 'Yoo-hoo!' in a high girlish voice and wave. Once I am sure Monkey Breath sees me, I am supposed to run like crazy."

Dusty patted Green Cheech on his green shoulder. "You're a good man, Green Cheech."

"And once I've done this, you swear I'll be in the inner circle, right?" Green Cheech asked.

"Dead center," said Dusty.

"Bull's-eye," said Wilson.

Green Cheech marched off down the hall to perform his mission. Melody said she had to go home, so we thanked her for her help and she left.

Wilson, Dusty, and I took off to the other side of the building where most of the lockers filled with empty soda cans were. Dusty led the way and Wilson and I followed.

"Have you ever seen Dusty so excited?" Wilson teased.

"Have you ever seen him walk this fast?" I joked.

"It's gonna work, dudes," Dusty said. "This is gonna be the scam of the century."

Just then Alice came around the corner.

Wilson stopped. "Correction. This *was* the scam of the century."

## 37

Alice's forehead was solid wrinkles. The corners of her mouth were turned down. When she saw us, her eyes narrowed with fury.

"What are you doing here?" she demanded.

"Uh, nothing," Dusty said.

Alice nodded. "Of course. Just hanging around wasting time. Meanwhile the rest of us are killing ourselves to try to scrape up every last can and bottle possible before the contest deadline."

"When's that again?" I asked.

Alice checked her watch. "At five o'clock, which is exactly fifteen minutes from now. A judge is coming with a truck to weigh everything. And we are going to lose, Kyle, thanks in no small part to you."

"Aw, gee, Alice, that's not nice," Dusty said.

"Maybe not," Alice sniffed. "But it's true. If Kyle and the rest of you had only helped, we'd probably be way ahead of Jeffersonville. Instead, my spies tell me we're at least fifty pounds be-hind."

"But think of all the good you've done even if we do lose," Wilson said. "I mean, all the stuff you've collected is just great for the environ-ment."

"Who gives a . . . " Alice started to say some-thing and then stopped. "Oh, what does it mat-ter?" She stormed off.

My friends and I watched her go.

"Know what she was going to say?" I asked.

"Who gives a hoot about the environment?" Wilson guessed.

"That's right," I said.

"So?" said Dusty. "That's no surprise. We always knew she was only in it because she has to win everything."

"I guess I just needed to be reminded," I said.

Dusty started walking again."Come on, we bet-ter get this over with," he said. "There's just too much going on around here."

We got to the lockers where the empty cans were stashed. Dusty took a box of big green plas-tic garbage bags out of his backpack. "Okay, fast, guys. We fill these bags with cans and then take 'em out behind the gym, across the field, and into the woods. We'll stash them there and then come back the next few nights and take a couple of bags at a time over to the Super Stop & Shop."

"Sounds like a plan." Wilson rubbed his hands together. "Let's get going."

Wilson and I went to work. Meanwhile, Dusty went into the gym to get the cans out of the empty gym lockers. We worked as fast as we could but it still took nearly twenty minutes to get all the cans into the bags. By the time Wilson and I were finished, we had six garbage bags filled to bursting with cans.

We were just finishing when Dusty came out of the gym dragging three more bulging bags.

"Okay, dudes, let's go!" he grunted.

Wilson and I each grabbed three bags. Along with Dusty, we started to drag all nine bags toward the exit.

"Hold it right there!" someone shouted.

My friends and I froze. We turned around. Coming up the hall toward us was Monkey Breath. And he was pulling Green Cheech by the dress collar.

# 38

Monkey Breath's clothes may have been in shreds, and his hair may have looked like it was loaded with static electricity, but his eyes were fierce and glaring.

"My, my, my," he chuckled. "Don't we look like we've been caught with our hands in the cookie jar."

My friends and I froze. We didn't know what to do. "What's in the bags, boys?" our principal asked.

"Er, what bags?" Dusty swallowed.

"That's lame, Dusty," Monkey Breath smirked. "Those nine large green garbage bags behind you."

"These bags?" Dusty was still trying to play dumb. But it was hopeless. Monkey Breath let go of Green Cheech and ripped open one of the bags. A dozen empty soda cans spilled out onto the floor.

Monkey Breath looked up with an evil grin on

his face. "Just as I suspected! You're the ones behind all those soda cans!"

My friends and I didn't know what to say. Meanwhile, you could almost see the gears churning around in Monkey Breath's demented head.

"Yes! It all makes sense now! You've been sneaking into the teachers' lounge! That violates *Rule #7: No student may enter the teachers' lounge without the official permission of the principal.* You've been buying sodas. That violates *Rule #1: The consumption of sweetened carbonated beverages during school hours is strictly forbidden.*" Monkey Breath paused and scratched his head. "The one thing I don't understand is how the four of you could have consumed so many sodas in so short a time."

"Oh, that's easy," said Green Cheech. "We didn't drink them all. We sold most of them to other kids."

Monkey Breath's jaw dropped. Wilson, Dusty, and I groaned.

"Did you really have to tell him that?" Dusty asked.

Green Cheech's eyes popped as he realized what he'd just done. "Oops!"

"Selling sodas?" Monkey Breath repeated gleefully. "Oh, that's good! That's *perfect*! That violates *Rule #62: No student may engage in commerce at any time on school property.*"

Our principal rubbed his hands together. "I've got you this time, boys! Do you understand? You've broken every rule in the book. This is great! I mean, this is bad for you! This goes beyond a month of detentions! Beyond suspension! Welcome, boys, to the land of expulsion!"

# 39

I'm not sure I'd ever seen Monkey Breath so happy. He insisted that we drag the bags of cans down to the office. As we pulled the bags down the hall behind him he muttered and mumbled about how glad he was to finally be getting rid of us.

My friends and I shared miserable looks.

Dusty was miserable because he knew he was going to lose all the returns money on those nine bags of cans.

Wilson was miserable because he figured we were finally going to be expelled.

I was miserable because it had really seemed like a great mission and now Monkey Breath had messed it all up.

This was the end. For once, Monkey Breath had really, truly nailed us. We were going down. And we weren't coming back.

Ahead of us, someone came around the corner.

It was probably the last person we wanted to see: Gary Gordon. When he saw us, he started to grin.

"Looks like you guys have been busted bad," he said with a leer.

"Get stuffed, Gary," Dusty grumbled.

"Sure, Dusty," Gary taunted. "I'll get stuffed. But I'll still be here at school. Looks like you'll be gone."

"That's enough, Gary," Monkey Breath said. "No gloating."

Gary stood there with a big grin on his face while my friends and I dragged the bags of cans past him. It was a clear shot down the hall to the office now. My friends and I trudged onward, dragging our bags and feeling like dead dudes walking.

All was lost.

We'd finally been nailed.

Our slogan, *We go where no rule has gone before,* would have to be rewritten.

We'd gone where the rules had gone before.

And we'd gotten busted.

Bad.

Then a group of people came around the corner.

The first person we saw was Alice. Her face was buried in her hands, and her shoulders trembled as if she were crying. Her friend Rachel Smath had her arm around Alice's shoulder to help guide her. Rachel's eyes were red and her cheeks were streaked with tears.

"Uh-oh, Alice is crying," Wilson muttered.

"We must have lost the recycling competition," said Dusty. "That's the only thing in the world that makes Alice cry."

Behind Alice was Ms. Fortune. Even our babe assistant principal was hanging her head, as if saddened by the loss.

Behind Ms. Fortune was a lady I'd never seen before.

She was very short.

She was carrying a clipboard.

And she was dressed all in green.

# 40

"Twenty-five pounds!" Alice was sobbing. "I can't believe we lost by twenty-five pounds!"

Suddenly, Rachel saw us and stopped. "Uh, Alice?"

But Alice was too deep in her misery to hear her friend. "And do you want to know why we lost?"

"Uh, Alice?" said Ms. Fortune.

"We lost because of Kyle Brawly!" Alice shrieked. "It's all *his* fault!"

"Alice," Ms. Fortune said firmly. "Shut up!"

At the sound of Ms. Fortune telling her to shut up, Alice opened her eyes.

Meanwhile, Monkey Breath's eyes were wide open, too. Only he wasn't looking at Alice, Rachel, or Ms. Fortune. He was staring at the lady in green.

"Oh, no!" he started to cry. "Oh, no!"

At the very same moment, Alice's eyes focused on the nine bulging green bags filled with soda cans.

"Oh, yes!" she cried. "Oh, yes!"

**41**

Well, as you probably figured out by now, nothing turned out the way any of us expected.

We never expected to help win the recycling competition, but thanks to those nine bags of soda cans, we did.

We never expected to be heroes, but since the nine bags of cans meant we won the competition, it also meant that because of us, everyone got to go to Big Splash Water Park for free.

It's hard to say whether Monkey Breath ever expected to come across a real little green woman, but he did. As far as we can tell, he never figured out that she was actually a judge for the recycling competition. Maybe it didn't matter. The last time we saw him, he was strapped flat on a gurney and being wheeled out of school by EMTs.

"Did you see her?" he was screaming. "Did you? She was green! I told you she'd be green!"

Ms. Fortune's our principal now. As a sort of symbolic gesture, she asked my friends and me to help her take the big metal door off Monkey Breath's office. We took out the metal detector and the soundproofing, too. And we were all there when Ms. Fortune opened the shades and let the sunlight in. The last thing she did was give each of us one of those big thick binders filled with school rules that Monkey Breath used to keep behind his desk.

"What should we do with them?" Wilson asked.

"Whatever you want, boys," she answered.

# 42

The bright yellow-and-orange flames from the bonfire rose high into the night sky. The orange sparks rose even higher before they drifted off into the dark and faded. The bonfire was part of the celebration that would continue the next day with our class trip to Big Splash Water Park.

My friends and I stood close enough to the fire to feel the heat. Each of us was holding one of Monkey Breath's big blue *School and Cafeteria Rules* binders.

"This is it, dudes," I said.

"Right," said Dusty. "And it's long overdue."

The sound of loud laughter caught our attention. Alice, Rachel, and their stuck-up popular friends were sitting in a circle listening to Cheech the Leech, who was telling them jokes.

"Hard to believe, huh?" Dusty said in a low voice they couldn't hear.

"Sure is," agreed Wilson.

111

What was hard to believe was that Cheech was not only Alice's new coanchor, but he was now one of the most popular boys in our grade. Being on TV had brought out a whole new side of Cheech.

"Oh, Cheech," Rachel gushed. "Do your imitation of Mr. Hush again."

Mr. Hush was our librarian.

"All right, girls," Cheech said in a perfect imitation of Mr. Hush's voice. "Enough talking. This isn't recess, it's serious study time."

The girls all cackled.

"Who would have thought he'd be so good at imitations?" Wilson wondered out loud.

"Kind of makes sense," I said. "He always did copy everyone."

Just then Alice stood up and started toward us.

"Uh-oh," Dusty whispered. "Here comes trouble."

Alice stepped in front of me.

"I just want to thank you again for helping us win the recycling competition, Kyle," she said.

"It really wasn't me," I said. "It was Dusty."

"Oh, you're just being modest," Alice replied with that gooey smile. "And I want to thank you for getting Cheech to be my coanchor. He's perfect."

"That wasn't my idea, either," I said.

Alice grinned. "You're so different, Kyle. Most

boys try to take credit for all the things they didn't do. You're the opposite."

"Not really," I said.

But you could see that Alice didn't hear a word I said. She just kept giving me that dreamy look.

"Anyway, I wanted to tell you that I've decided you're right," she said. "I am way too competitive. Now that we've won the recycling competition I've decided to tone it way down."

"That's, er, great," I said, not sure I really believed her.

"Well, see you tomorrow." Alice smiled and went back to her friends.

I turned back to my friends. "Ready, guys?"

"Ready," answered Wilson and Dusty.

"Hold it." Ms. Fortune came through the dark toward us. "What are you going to do with those binders?"

"Throw them into the fire, what else?" Dusty answered.

Our new principal's red lips turned down into a frown. "Do you really think you should?"

"You said we could do anything we wanted with them," Wilson reminded her.

"You're right, I did," Ms. Fortune said. "All right, boys, but you promise you won't sell any more sodas in school?"

"We promise," we said.

"Have fun." Ms. Fortune turned away.

"Okay, dudes, let's do it," I said. "One, two, three!"

We threw the binders into the fire. They disappeared into the flames, and a huge splash of orange sparks burst into the sky above.

"That's it, dudes," I said. "The end of the evil empire of Dr. Monkey Breath."

"Should we say our motto?" Wilson asked.

"Doesn't seem like it's necessary," Dusty said. "Now that Monkey Breath's gone."

"One last time?" Wilson begged. "Just for old times' sake?"

"Sure, why not?" I said.

We chanted our motto, *We go where no rules have gone before,* and slapped palms. We were free. From now on, the only rules at Hard Marks Middle School would be normal rules.

The flames from the bonfire reached high into the dark sky. I wondered if Monkey Breath could see them, too, from his padded cell wherever he was.

Hi, this is Cheech. Formerly Cheech the Leech, but now Cheech the def cool dude and official member of the inner circle. In the last three books, Kyle, Dusty, and Wilson each got to tell you some cool stuff to do. Now it's my turn.

First of all, I'm sure you know that you don't want to sell or buy stuff in the boys' room. Go to a store instead. I promise you, most stores will smell better.

So here's a cool thing you can do if you have a pet snake, guinea pig, mouse, rabbit, lizard, or frog. Hold your pet in your hand so that it's resting on its back. Then rub your finger up and down its stomach. Not too hard. Just nice and soft. Chances are good you can put that pet into a trance. It'll just lie there like it's totally spaced out.

You should try it. It's really cool. Warning: It doesn't work on cats, dogs, or turtles. And you weirdos who have pet cockroaches can forget about it, too.

Kyle says it'll probably work on Gary Gordon. So if you see him around, you might give it a try. And let me know how it works.

# About the Author

Todd Strasser has written many award-winning novels for young and teenage readers. Among his best-known books are *Help! I'm Trapped in Obedience School* and *Help! I'm Trapped in Santa's Body*. His most recent books for Scholastic are *Help! I'm Trapped in a Supermodel's Body* and *Help! I'm Trapped in a Professional Wrestler's Body*.

The movie *Drive Me Crazy*, starring Melissa Joan Hart, was based on his novel *How I Created My Perfect Prom Date*.

Todd speaks frequently at schools about the craft of writing and conducts writing workshops for young people. He and his family live outside New York City with their yellow Labrador retriever, Mac.

You can find out more about Todd and his books at http://www.toddstrasser.com

## READ ALL THE HILARIOUS BOOKS IN THE

## SERIES
## BY TODD STRASSER

### DON'T GET CAUGHT DRIVING THE SCHOOL BUS

There's a new driver on the bus route. Sarge used to work at a prison, and he treats all the kids like they're criminals. But Kyle and his friends show Sarge who's really in charge!

### DON'T GET CAUGHT WEARING THE LUNCH LADY'S HAIRNET

Food fights in the cafeteria are raging out of control, so Principal Chump hires some psycho lunch monitors to bust up the trouble. Armed with dishrags, hairnets, and a hidden camera, Kyle and the boys are about to strike back.

### DON'T GET CAUGHT IN THE GIRLS LOCKER ROOM

There's a rumor that the girls keep a Kissing Book in their locker room. The girls write about guys in it. How they kiss and stuff. Kyle, Wilson, and Dusty find out that the girls have trash-talked them in the book. So the boys decide to steal it . . .

# READ ALL THE BOOKS BASED ON THE HIT TV SHOW!